STORIES FROM THE RIDESHARE DRIVER'S SEAT

REAL PEOPLE. REAL MOMENTS. REAL RIDES.

(FICTIONAL STORIES INSPIRED BY THE TRUTH OF THE ROAD)

BY

WHISKY BLU

Stories From The Rideshare Driver's Seat – Volume I Whisky Blu Real People. Real Moments. Real Stories.

CONTENTS

PART I — THE ROAD OPENS

CHAPTER ONE – THE GCAP RIDE

Where purpose first whispers — a ride that plants the seed of a vision much bigger than the moment.

CHAPTER TWO – THE FAMILY THAT LET GO RIDE

A tender encounter with a family learning to release what they cannot control.

CHAPTER THREE – THE STROKE SURVIVOR RIDE

A story of resilience, determination, and the quiet fight to reclaim one's life.

CHAPTER FOUR – THE LEFT BEHIND LUGGAGE RIDE

A simple mistake becomes a window into grief, memory, and what we carry without meaning to.

CHAPTER FIVE – THE BIRTHDAY RIDE

A celebration wrapped in loneliness — and the unexpected gift of being seen.

FOREWORD

There are storytellers… and then there are witnesses.

Whisky Blu is both.

Most people move through the world without ever truly seeing the lives around them. They pass strangers on sidewalks, sit beside them in waiting rooms, stand behind them in grocery lines — never knowing the battles being fought just beneath the surface. But some people are built differently. Some people are wired to listen, to notice, to hold space for the stories others are afraid to speak.

Whisky Blu is one of those rare souls.

What began as a rideshare job became something far more profound — a ministry without walls, a sanctuary on wheels, a moving confessional where truth could breathe. In the quiet hum of the engine, in the glow of dashboard lights, people found the courage to share the parts of themselves they'd hidden from the world. And Whisky, with his steady presence and open heart, became the keeper of those moments.

This book is not just a collection of stories.

It is a testament.

A testament to resilience.

To humanity.

To the sacredness of being seen.

Every chapter in these pages carries the heartbeat of someone who stepped into Whisky's car carrying more than luggage. They carried grief, hope, secrets, diagnoses, dreams, trauma, faith, identity, and the fragile pieces of themselves they weren't sure anyone would understand.

And somehow, in the span of a ride, they found understanding.

Whisky doesn't sensationalize their stories.

He honors them.

He protects them.

He transforms them into narratives that remind us of something we often forget:

Every person living a life you know nothing about.

These stories — fictionalized for privacy, but rooted in truth — are mirrors.

They reflect the world as it is: messy, beautiful, painful, hopeful, complicated, and deeply human.

And just when you think you've reached the end of what one book can hold… Whisky gives you a final story that opens a door into something bigger. Something darker. Something that promises.

So take a breath.

Settle in.

And prepare yourself.

Because once you step into the passenger seat of Whisky Blu's world, you won't leave the same way you came.

Bishop Anthon F. Burgess

DEDICATION

This book is dedicated to the people who ride quietly, who carry stories in their eyes, who fight battles no one sees, and who still choose to keep going.

To the ones who have been overlooked, unheard, misunderstood, yet continue to show up for life with courage that deserves to be honored.

To every survivor, every dreamer, every soul rebuilding themselves one mile, one moment, one breath at a time.

To the strangers who became teachers, the riders who became reminders, and the voices that stayed with me long after the doors closed.

And to anyone who has ever felt alone on their journey — may these stories remind you that your truth matters, your story is sacred, and your life is worth the ride.

ACKNOWLEDGMENTS

To every rider who ever stepped into my car carrying more than luggage — thank you. Your courage, your honesty, and your willingness to share a piece of your life made this book possible. These stories may be fictionalized, but the humanity behind them is real, and it belongs to you.

To the people who taught me that listening is a form of love — the elders, the strangers, the broken, the healed, the ones who whispered their truth in the dark and the ones who spoke it boldly in the light — I honor you.

To those who believed in me when life felt heavy, who reminded me that purpose can be found in unexpected places, and who encouraged me to keep going even when the road was rough — your faith carried me farther than you know.

To the communities that shaped me, the ones that welcomed me, and even the ones that rejected me — you all played a part in the man I've become. Your lessons, your love, and your losses live between these pages.

To the people fighting silent battles — illness, identity, grief, trauma, reinvention — this book is for you. May these stories remind you that you are not alone, that your truth matters, and that your journey is worthy of being told.

And finally, to the road itself — for being my classroom, my sanctuary, my mirror, and my ministry. Thank you for every mile, every moment, and every story that found its way into my hands.

AUTHOR'S NOTE

I didn't set out to write a book. I set out to survive. And somewhere between the miles, the midnight pickups, the quiet riders, and the unexpected conversations, I realized I was witnessing something sacred — the everyday humanity most people never slow down long enough to see.

These stories are fictional, but the heartbeat behind them is real. They were born from the road, from the people who stepped into my car carrying joy, grief, secrets, hope, and sometimes nothing but exhaustion.

Every ride reminded me that no matter who we are or where we come from, we are all navigating something. We are all trying to get somewhere — physically, emotionally, spiritually.

Driving gave me a front-row seat to the truth: People don't need judgment. They need space. They need dignity. They need to be seen.

This book is my way of honoring the riders who unknowingly became teachers, mirrors, and reminders.

It is also a tribute to the journey I've walked — through caregiving, through homelessness, through rebuilding, through rediscovering myself one mile at a time.

I wrote these stories with love, respect, and a deep commitment to the humanity that connects us. If you find yourself in these pages — in the silence, in the struggle, in the laughter, or in the healing — know that you are not alone. Your story matters. Your journey matters. And you deserve to be carried with care.

Thank you for riding with me.

INTRODUCTION

Every rideshare driver has a route. Mine just happened to lead me through some of the most unexpected classrooms life could offer.

When I first sat behind the wheel, I thought I was simply driving people from one place to another. But the road has a way of revealing truth. It shows you who people are when they think no one is paying attention. It shows you who *you* are when you're forced to sit with your own thoughts between rides. And it shows you how much humanity still exists in a world that often forgets to slow down long enough to notice it.

This book is a collection of stories inspired by the moments that stayed with me — the quiet ones, the heavy ones, the healing ones, the ones that reminded me that every person carries a universe inside them. Some of these stories reflect real conversations. Others reflect the emotions, lessons, and truths I witnessed along the way. All of them honor the dignity of the people who stepped into my car, even if only for a few minutes.

Driving gives me a front-row seat to the resilience of everyday people. The single mother holding her family together with sheer will. The elder fighting through illness with grace. The person rebuilding their life one appointment, one paycheck, one breath at a time. The ones who laugh to keep from crying. The ones who cry because they finally feel safe enough to let go.

These rides taught me that healing doesn't always happen in big moments. Sometimes it happens in the backseat of a car at 6 a.m., or during a late-night ride when the world is quiet enough for truth to speak.

Volume I is the beginning of a larger journey — a series that captures the humanity I've witnessed mile after mile. My hope is that as you read, you don't just see the characters. You see yourself. You see your neighbor. You see the people you pass every day without knowing what they're carrying.

These stories are an invitation: to slow down, to listen deeper, to hold space for others, and to remember that every life has value, even when the world overlooks it.

Welcome to the passenger seat of my journey. Welcome to the stories that changed me. Welcome to *Stories From The Rideshare Driver's Seat – Volume I.*

PART I — THE ROAD OPENS

CHAPTER ONE: THE GCAP RIDE

The request came in from a quiet street on the north end of town — the kind of place where the houses look tired, like they've seen too many winters.

Whisky Blu pulled up to the curb and saw a man sitting on the steps, a duffel bag at his feet, shoulders slumped like the world had been riding him instead of the other way around.

He stood when the car approached.

"You Whisky?" he asked, voice low.

"Yeah, brother. You headed to GCAP?"

The man nodded, eyes drifting toward the bag at his feet.

"That's all I got left," he said. "But they said they got a bed for me tonight."

Whisky popped the trunk. "Then let's get you there."

The man climbed in, staring out the window as the neighborhood rolled by.

A few minutes into the ride, he spoke again.

"I ain't never asked for help before. Always been the one helping everybody else. But life… life flipped on me fast."

Whisky nodded. "Happens quicker than people think."

The man swallowed hard.

"Lost my job. Lost my place. Lost my people. I've been sleeping behind the old laundromat for three nights. I'm just… tired, man."

Whisky didn't rush him.

Didn't try to fix it.

Just let the silence breathe.

"They told me GCAP ain't just a shelter," the man said. "Said it's a place where folks actually care."

Whisky smiled. "They do. They really do."

As they got closer, the man leaned forward, watching the building come into view — warm lights glowing through the windows, people moving inside with purpose, not pity.

"That it?" he asked softly.

"That's it," Whisky said. "A fresh start behind those doors."

When they pulled up, the man didn't move right away.

 He sat there, breathing, gathering himself.

"You know," he said, "I thought this ride was gonna feel like the end of something. But it doesn't. Feels like... maybe the beginning."

Whisky turned in his seat.

"Brother, sometimes the hardest step is the one through the front door. But once you take it... everything else is just healing."

The man nodded, eyes shining.

"Thank you," he whispered. "For treating me like I'm still somebody."

"You are somebody," Whisky said. "And GCAP's gonna help you remember that."

The man stepped out, grabbed his bag, and walked toward the entrance — shoulders still heavy, but no longer dragging.

Whisky watched him go, knowing this ride wasn't just transportation.

It was a transition.

It was hope.

It was the moment a man decided he wasn't done yet.

Some rides take people across town.

Others… take them back to themselves.

CHAPTER TWO: THE FAMILY THAT LET GO

The request came in just after sunset — a pickup from a neighborhood where the houses sat close together, but the people inside them felt miles apart.

Whisky Blu pulled up to a small brick home with the porch light flickering like it couldn't decide whether to stay on.

A woman stepped outside, dragging a suitcase that looked heavier than it should've been.

Not because of what was inside…

but because of what she was leaving behind.

She opened the door and slid into the back seat, wiping her face quickly like she didn't want anyone to see the tears.

"You Whisky?" she asked, voice tight.

"Yes, ma'am," he said softly. "Where we headed?"

She hesitated.

"Anywhere but here."

Whisky nodded.

"Alright. We'll drive until you're ready."

They pulled away from the curb, the house shrinking in the rearview mirror like a chapter closing itself.

A few minutes into the ride, she spoke — voice trembling but steadying with each word.

"My family told me today… I'm no longer welcome.

Said I'm 'too much.'

Said I'm a burden.

Said I should figure life out on my own."

Whisky didn't interrupt.

Didn't rush her.

Just let her speak.

She continued.

"I've been helping them for years.

Taking care of everybody.

Showing up for everybody.

But the moment I needed help…

they shut the door."

Whisky nodded slowly.

"That kind of hurt cuts deep."

She looked up, surprised by the understanding.

"It's like… I always knew they didn't really see me.

But hearing it out loud?

Hearing your own blood say you're disposable?"

She shook her head.

"It breaks something inside you."

Whisky's voice was calm, grounded.

"Sometimes family is DNA.

And sometimes family is the people who choose you."

She let out a breath — shaky, but freeing.

"You know what's crazy?" she said.

"I'm scared… but I also feel lighter.

Like maybe this is the first step toward a life that's actually mine."

Whisky nodded.

"Painful beginnings still lead to new beginnings."

As they approached the edge of town, she leaned forward.

"Can you take me to the hotel near the highway?

Just for tonight.

Tomorrow… I'll figure out the rest."

Whisky pulled in gently.

Before she got out, she paused.

"Thank you," she whispered.

"For not asking what I did wrong.

For not judging me.

For just… letting me be."

Whisky met her eyes in the mirror.

"You didn't do anything wrong.

Some people can't handle the weight of their own shortcomings,

so they put it on the person who's strongest."

She swallowed hard — not from sadness, but from recognition.

"You're right," she said softly.

"And I'm done carrying what isn't mine."

She stepped out, suitcase rolling behind her — not dragging this time, but moving with purpose.

Whisky watched her walk toward the lobby, shoulders still tender but no longer bowed.

Some rides carry people away from home.

Others carry people toward themselves.

And sometimes… leaving is the first act of healing.

CHAPTER THREE: THE STROKE SURVIVOR RIDE

The request came in early — the kind of early where the sun is still deciding whether it wants to rise.

Whisky Blu pulled up to a small apartment complex, expecting a routine morning ride to work.

Instead, the door opened slowly… and a man stepped out with careful, deliberate movements.

One hand gripping a cane.

The other holding the railing like it was an old friend.

He made his way to the car, pausing once to catch his balance.

Whisky got out and opened the door for him.

"Take your time, brother," he said gently.

The man nodded, breath steady but effortful.

"Appreciate you. I'm headed to therapy… again."

He settled into the seat, adjusting his leg with both hands.

A few minutes into the ride, he spoke.

"Six months ago, I couldn't even lift my arm. Couldn't talk right. Couldn't walk.

Doctors said I might not get much back."

Whisky glanced at him in the mirror.

"But you're getting it back."

The man smiled — small, but real.

"I'm trying. Every day. Folks think recovery is just physical therapy. But it's the mental part that gets you.

Waking up in a body that doesn't move the way you remember.

Trying to say a word you've said your whole life… and it gets stuck."

Whisky nodded slowly.

"I know that road."

The man looked up, surprised.

"You do?"

Whisky didn't go into detail — didn't need to.

"Yeah. I do."

Silence filled the car, but it wasn't heavy.

It was understanding.

The man exhaled.

"People treat you differently after a stroke. Like you're fragile. Or broken.

But I'm still me. Just… rebuilding."

Whisky smiled.

"Rebuilding is still progress."

As they approached the therapy center, the man straightened up, determination settling into his shoulders.

"You know what my therapist told me yesterday?" he said.

"She said every step counts — even the ugly ones."

Whisky chuckled.

"She's right."

When they pulled up, the man didn't get out immediately.

He looked at Whisky with clear, steady eyes.

"Thank you," he said.

"For not rushing me. For not talking to me like I'm less."

Whisky nodded.

"Brother, surviving a stroke doesn't make you less.

It makes you a fighter."

The man smiled — wider this time — and stepped out of the car, cane tapping the pavement like a drumbeat of resilience.

Whisky watched him walk toward the entrance, each step slow… but each step his.

Some rides carry people to appointments.

Others carry them back to their strength.

CHAPTER FOUR: THE LEFT-BEHIND LUGGAGE RIDE

The ping came just after midnight — airport pickup, Terminal C.

Whisky Blu pulled up to the curb, expecting a tired traveler, maybe a business suit or a college kid heading home.

Instead, he saw a woman standing alone with one suitcase… and eyes that looked like she'd been holding her breath for hours.

She slid into the back seat slowly, like her body was moving but her spirit was still catching up.

"Evening," Whisky said gently.

She nodded. "Hi… sorry. It's been a day."

They pulled away from the terminal, the glow of the airport fading behind them.

A few minutes into the ride, she spoke again — voice trembling but trying to stay steady.

"I flew here to surprise my fiancé."

A pause.

"He wasn't there."

Whisky didn't say a word. He just listened — the kind of listening that lets someone unravel safely.

"He left. Just… left. No note. No explanation. His roommate said he moved out last week."

She laughed, but it wasn't joy.

"I crossed three states for a man who didn't even stay long enough to say goodbye."

Silence filled the car, but it wasn't empty. It was the kind that holds someone together.

Whisky finally said, "Sometimes the road brings us where we didn't expect… but exactly where we need to be."

She wiped her eyes. "I don't even know where I'm going now."

"You're going forward," he said. "One mile at a time."

When they reached her hotel, she hesitated before getting out.

"Thank you," she whispered. "You're the first person today who didn't make me feel stupid."

Whisky nodded. "Heartbreak doesn't make you foolish. It makes you human."

She stepped out, pulling her single suitcase behind her — the only thing she had left of a trip meant to change her life.

And as she walked toward the lobby, Whisky knew:

Some rides aren't about the destination.

They're about helping someone find their way back to themselves.

CHAPTER FIVE: THE BIRTHDAY RIDE

It was a slow afternoon when the request came in — a pickup from a small brick house on the east side.

Whisky Blu pulled up expecting the usual: someone heading to work, to the store, to life.

Instead, the door opened and out came a little boy — maybe eight years old — dressed in his Sunday best.

Behind him stood an older woman, probably his grandmother, holding a small gift bag and smiling like she was holding back tears.

She leaned into the window.

"Sir… could you make sure he gets to the bowling alley on Prospect? It's his birthday party. His mama's working a double, and I can't drive anymore."

Whisky nodded. "I got him."

The boy climbed in, legs swinging, eyes bright but nervous.

"You like bowling?" Whisky asked.

He shrugged. "I've never been. Mama said maybe next year… but Grandma said this year is my year."

Whisky smiled. "Well then, today's the day."

As they drove, the boy talked about superheroes, school lunch, and how he hoped at least one friend would show up.

Whisky listened — really listened — the way kids can tell when someone actually cares.

When they pulled up to the bowling alley, the boy froze.

Only one kid was there.

 One.

A classmate holding a small wrapped box, looking just as unsure.

The boy whispered, "At least somebody came."

Whisky put a hand on the seat and said, "Hey… one real friend is worth a room full of fake ones."

The boy nodded, took a breath, and stepped out.

Before he ran inside, he turned back.

"Thank you for the ride, Mister Whisky. You made me feel like today is my year."

Whisky watched him join his friend — two kids, one lane, and a birthday that suddenly didn't look so small.

Some rides are short.

 Some rides are simple.

 But some rides… remind you that joy doesn't need a crowd.

CHAPTER SIX: THE NIGHTLY DIALYSIS RIDE

The request came in just after sunset — that in-between hour when the sky is still blue but the streetlights are already humming.

Whisky Blu pulled up to a small duplex, expecting a routine ride to the store or a friend's house.

Instead, the door opened, and a man stepped out carrying a medical supply bag — the kind you only recognize if you've lived around it.

He moved slowly, carefully, like every step had to be negotiated with his body.

"You Whisky?" he asked.

Whisky nodded. "Yes, sir. Headed to the clinic?"

The man shook his head.

"Nah… I'm on peritoneal dialysis. Do it at home. I'm just going to pick up my supplies. They finally came in."

He eased into the back seat, adjusting himself with practiced patience.

A few minutes into the ride, he spoke again.

"People think dialysis is just a machine. But it's a whole life.

Every night. Every single night.

Hook up, drain, fill, repeat.

While the world sleeps… I'm fighting to stay alive."

Whisky nodded gently.

"I hear you."

The man looked up, surprised.

"You know about this?"

Whisky didn't explain — didn't need to.

"Yeah. I know."

The man exhaled, a mix of relief and exhaustion.

"CKD takes everything slow. Your energy. Your appetite. Your freedom.

But PD… PD gives you a little bit back. Let you stay home.

Let's you keep some dignity."

Whisky nodded.

"And it takes strength most folks never see."

The man smiled — tired, but proud.

"Some nights I wanna quit. But then I remember… quitting ain't an option.

I got people who still need me.

And I ain't done yet."

As they pulled up to the supply center, he leaned forward.

"You know what's funny?" he said.

"People look at me and see sickness.

But they don't see the fight.

They don't see the discipline.

They don't see the courage it takes to hook up to a machine every night and still wake up grateful."

Whisky met his eyes in the mirror.

"They don't see it… but I do."

The man swallowed hard.

"Thank you," he whispered. "For treating me like I'm more than my condition."

Whisky nodded.

"You are. And every night you hook up… you're proving it."

The man stepped out, lifting his supply bag with steady hands — not strong hands, but determined ones.

Whisky watched him walk inside, knowing this ride wasn't about illness.

It was about endurance.

About choosing life again and again, even when it hurts.

Some rides carry people to appointments.

Others carry people through battles no one else can see.

CHAPTER SEVEN: THE QUIET MIND RIDE

The request came in mid-morning — a pickup from a small counseling center tucked between a laundromat and a corner store.

Whisky Blu pulled up and saw a woman standing outside, arms wrapped around herself, even though the weather was warm.

She opened the door gently and slid into the back seat.

"You Whisky?" she asked softly.

"Yes, ma'am," he said. "Where to?"

She hesitated.

"Home… I think. Or maybe the park. I haven't decided yet."

Whisky nodded.

"No rush. We'll figure it out."

They pulled away from the curb, the hum of the engine filling the quiet.

A few minutes into the ride, she spoke — voice trembling but honest.

"I had a rough session today. My therapist says I'm doing better, but… my mind doesn't always agree."

Whisky nodded slowly.

"I hear you."

She looked up, surprised.

"You ever dealt with anxiety? Depression? Anything like that?"

Whisky didn't explain — didn't need to.

"Yeah. I've seen those storms."

She exhaled, a breath that sounded like it had been held for days.

"People think mental illness is just sadness. Or nerves.

But it's not.

It's waking up and fighting your own thoughts before you even brush your teeth.

It's trying to look normal when your brain is screaming.

It's surviving a battle nobody else can see."

Whisky nodded.

"That's real strength."

She wiped her eyes.

"I take my meds. I go to therapy. I do the work.

But some days… some days I feel like I'm made of glass."

Whisky glanced at her in the mirror.

"Glass still reflects light."

She smiled — small, but genuine.

"You know… I almost canceled my appointment today.

But I didn't.

And that counts for something."

"It counts for a lot," Whisky said.

As they approached the park, she leaned forward.

"Can we stop here? I just… I need a minute with the trees. They don't judge."

Whisky pulled over gently.

Before she got out, she paused.

"Thank you," she whispered.

 "For not treating me like I'm broken."

Whisky shook his head.

"You're not broken.

 You're healing.

 And healing takes courage."

She stepped out, walking toward a bench under a tall oak tree — shoulders still heavy, but her steps steady.

Whisky watched her go, knowing this ride wasn't about distance.

 It was about giving someone space to breathe.

Some rides carry people across town.

 Others carry people through the weight of their own minds.

 And sometimes… that's the most important ride of all.

CHAPTER EIGHT: THE ONE-DAY-AT-A-TIME RIDE

The request came in just after noon — a pickup from a community center on the west side.

Whisky Blu pulled up and saw a man standing outside, hands in his pockets, rocking gently on his heels like he was trying to settle his nerves.

He climbed in slowly.

"You Whisky?" he asked.

"Yes sir," Whisky replied. "Where we headed?"

The man gave a small smile.

"Home. Well… halfway home. I'm in sober living."

Whisky nodded.

"Alright. Let's get you there."

They pulled off, the hum of the engine filling the space between them.

A few minutes into the ride, the man spoke again.

"I just came from my meeting. Ninety days clean today."

He paused.

"Feels weird saying that out loud."

Whisky glanced at him in the mirror.

"Ninety days is something to be proud of."

The man let out a breath — shaky, but steady.

"Yeah… I'm trying. But recovery ain't pretty. Folks think it's just quitting.

But it's relearning everything.

How to feel.

How to cope.

How to sit with yourself without running."

Whisky nodded.

"I hear that."

The man looked up, surprised.

"You been around recovery before?"

Whisky didn't explain — didn't need to.

"Yeah. I've seen the fight."

The man nodded slowly, comforted by the understanding.

"You know what's wild?" he said.

"People treat addiction like it's a moral failure.

But nobody wakes up one day and chooses to destroy their life.

Most of us were just trying to numb something we didn't know how to face."

Whisky nodded.

"Pain makes people reach for whatever's closest."

The man smiled — small, but real.

"But I'm learning now.

Learning to sit with the pain.

Learning to breathe through the cravings.

Learning that I'm worth the work."

As they approached the sober living house, the man leaned forward.

"My sponsor told me something today," he said.

"She said, 'Recovery isn't about perfection. It's about direction.'

And for the first time… I feel like I'm pointed the right way."

Whisky pulled up to the curb and turned toward him.

"You're doing the hardest part," he said.

"You're showing up for yourself."

The man swallowed hard.

"Thank you," he whispered.

"For treating me like a person.

Not a problem."

Whisky nodded.

"You're not a problem.

You're a survivor."

The man stepped out, shoulders straighter, steps more certain — a man rebuilding his life one day, one choice, one breath at a time.

Some rides carry people home.

Others carry people toward the version of themselves they're fighting to become.

CHAPTER NINE: THE UNDETECTABLE RIDE

The request came in late afternoon — that golden hour when sunlight makes everything look softer than it really is.

Whisky Blu pulled up to a quiet apartment building, expecting a quick ride across town.

The door opened, and a man stepped out wearing a simple backpack and a calm smile.

He looked healthy, steady, grounded — the kind of person who carried his life with quiet confidence.

He slid into the back seat.

"You Whisky?" he asked.

"Yes sir," Whisky replied. "Headed to the clinic?"

The man nodded.

"Yeah. Just my routine check-in. Nothing dramatic."

They pulled off, the city rolling by in warm light.

A few minutes into the ride, the man spoke again.

"You know… people hear the word HIV and think it's a death sentence.

But I'm healthier now than I was in my twenties."

Whisky nodded.

"I've heard that from a lot of folks. Medicine's come a long way."

The man smiled — not proud, just real.

"I've been undetectable for eight years.

Take my meds every day.

Live my life.

Work my job.

Love who I love.

I'm still me."

Whisky glanced at him in the mirror.

"That's how it should be."

The man exhaled — not heavy, just honest.

"What gets me," he said, "is the stigma.

People don't understand science.

They don't understand U=U.

They don't understand that I'm not a threat to anybody.

I'm just a man living his life."

Whisky nodded slowly.

"People fear what they don't know.

But fear don't change facts."

The man chuckled.

"Exactly. I tell folks:

'I'm not dangerous.

I'm disciplined.'

And that discipline keeps me alive."

As they neared the clinic, he leaned forward.

"You know what I wish?" he said.

"I wish people understood that HIV isn't who I am.

It's just something I manage.

Like diabetes.

Like high blood pressure.

Like anything else."

Whisky nodded.

"You're not your diagnosis.

You're your resilience."

The man smiled — wide this time.

"Thank you," he said softly.

"For seeing me.

Not the letters."

Whisky pulled up to the entrance.

"Brother," he said, "you're living proof that life doesn't end with HIV.

It just changes.

And you're handling that change like a champion."

The man stepped out, adjusting his backpack, shoulders relaxed and steady.

Whisky watched him walk toward the clinic — not ashamed, not afraid, just living.

Some rides carry people to appointments.

Others carry people through the weight of misunderstanding.

But this one…This one carried truth.

CHAPTER TEN: THE BACKPACK RIDE

It was cold — the kind of cold that makes the night feel heavier than it should.

Whisky Blu pulled into the pickup spot behind a grocery store, a place where rides usually meant late-night workers heading home.

But tonight, a man stepped out from the shadows.

Thin jacket.

Worn shoes.

A single backpack held tight to his chest like it was the last thing he owned.

He opened the door slowly.

"You Whisky?" he asked.

Whisky nodded. "Hop in, brother. Warm in here."

The man settled into the back seat, rubbing his hands together over the heater vents.

"Appreciate it," he said. "Been outside a while."

Whisky didn't pry.

Didn't stare.

Just drove.

A few minutes passed before the man spoke again.

"I'm headed to the shelter on Walnut. They only take folks until ten. I'm cutting it close."

Whisky checked the time.

They'd make it — but barely.

"You good?" Whisky asked gently.

The man let out a breath that sounded like it had been trapped in him for days.

"Lost my job. Lost my place. Lost my people. But I ain't lost my hope. Not yet."

Whisky nodded. "Hope's the one thing nobody can repossess."

The man chuckled — a tired, grateful sound.

"You sound like a preacher," he said.

Whisky smiled. "Just a man who's seen some things."

As they neared the shelter, the man leaned forward.

"You know… most drivers look at me like I'm trouble. Like I'm dirt. You didn't."

Whisky met his eyes in the mirror.

"Everybody's somebody. And everybody's story matters."

The man swallowed hard.

"Thank you… for treating me like a person."

When they pulled up, he hesitated before getting out.

"If I get back on my feet… I'm gonna remember this ride."

Whisky nodded.

"You already took the first step. The rest is just miles."

The man slung his backpack over his shoulder and walked toward the shelter door — shoulders straighter, steps steadier, hope still intact.

Some rides don't change the world.

But they can change a night.

And sometimes… that's enough.

PART II — THE FINAL ARC

CHAPTER ELEVEN: THE PINK RIBBON RIDE

The request came in early morning — the kind of morning where the sky is still deciding whether it wants to be blue or gray.

Whisky Blu pulled up to a small townhouse on the east side.

The porch light was on, even though the sun had already risen.

A woman stepped outside, moving slowly but with purpose.

She wore a soft pink headwrap, a denim jacket, and a smile that tried to hide the exhaustion beneath it.

She opened the door and eased into the back seat.

"You Whisky?" she asked gently.

"Yes ma'am," he said. "Where we headed?"

She took a breath.

"The cancer center. Treatment day."

Whisky nodded.

"Alright. We'll get you there."

They pulled off, the morning quiet settling around them like a blanket.

A few minutes into the ride, she spoke — voice steady, but carrying the weight of someone who'd had to be strong for too long.

"You know… people think breast cancer is just about losing your hair.

But it's not.

It's losing your energy.

Your appetite.

Your sense of normal.

Sometimes even your sense of yourself."

Whisky nodded slowly.

"I hear that."

She looked out the window, watching the world pass by.

"I used to be a teacher," she said.

"Third grade.

I loved those kids.

But chemo… it takes more than your strength.

It takes your rhythm.

Your routine.

Your ability to pretend everything's fine."

Whisky listened — not with pity, but with presence.

She continued.

"My family tries to help.

But they're scared.

They don't know what to say.

Sometimes I feel like I'm comforting them more than they're comforting me."

Whisky nodded.

"That happens more than people realize."

She smiled — small, but real.

"But you know what I've learned?" she said.

"Cancer doesn't get to define me.

It doesn't get to take my joy.

It doesn't get to decide how my story ends."

Her voice grew stronger.

"I'm still here.

Still fighting.

Still waking up every morning choosing hope."

As they approached the cancer center, she leaned forward.

"Can you stop right by the front door?

Some days the walk feels longer than it looks."

Whisky pulled in gently.

Before she stepped out, she paused.

"Thank you," she said softly.

"For treating me like a person… not a diagnosis."

Whisky met her eyes in the mirror.

"You're not your cancer.

You're your courage."

She swallowed hard — not from fear, but from recognition.

"Yeah," she whispered.

"I guess I am."

She stepped out, adjusting her pink headwrap, shoulders squared, steps steady — a woman fighting for her life with grace, grit, and a quiet kind of power.

Whisky watched her walk toward the entrance, knowing this ride wasn't about getting her to treatment.

It was about reminding her she wasn't alone.

Some rides carry people to appointments.

Others carry people through the hardest chapters of their lives.

And sometimes… they carry hope.

CHAPTER TWELVE: THE RIDE THAT PULLED ME BACK — AND STAYED

Some days start heavy for no clear reason. This was one of those days.

I was frustrated, worn down, and carrying a sadness I couldn't shake. Nothing dramatic had happened — just the slow build of too many responsibilities, too many disappointments, too many moments where I felt like I was giving more than I had left. I was driving, but my spirit wasn't in the car with me.

Then the request came in.

Pickup: *Residential address.* Notes: *Passenger uses a wheelchair.*

I almost didn't accept it. Not because of him — but because I didn't feel like I had anything left to give. But something in me said, *Go anyway.*

When I pulled up, the door opened and a man rolled out in a wheelchair. Both of his legs were gone — but his smile was whole, warm, and steady.

"Appreciate you coming, brother," he said.

I helped him into the car, folded his chair, and placed it in the trunk. He apologized for taking a little extra time. I told him it was fine, but inside, I was unraveling.

A few minutes into the ride, he looked at me through the mirror.

"You alright up there?"

I hadn't said a word about my day. But somehow, he saw straight through me.

"I'm hanging in there," I said quietly.

He nodded, then spoke with the calm wisdom of someone who had lived through storms.

"I used to have days like that, too. Days where I thought I couldn't take one more thing. Then life took my legs… and somehow gave me a new reason to live."

He wasn't trying to inspire me. He wasn't performing strength. He was simply telling the truth.

"You know what kept me going?" he continued. "I realized I still had purpose. Even when I couldn't see it. Even when it didn't feel like it. I was still here. And being here means there's more ahead than behind."

His words hit me deeper than he knew.

He didn't know the weight I was carrying. He didn't know how close I felt to giving up on myself. He didn't know he was speaking life into someone who desperately needed it.

But he was.

When we arrived, I helped him back into his chair. He looked at me with a steady, knowing gaze.

"Whatever you're carrying, don't carry it alone. And don't give up on yourself. You matter more than you think."

He rolled away, but something in me stayed with him.

I sat in the car afterward, quiet, breathing, letting his words settle into the places that hurt.

That ride didn't just shift my day. It shifted my life.

And here's the part I didn't know then:

That man — that stranger who spoke truth into me when I needed it most — would become one of my closest friends. A brother. A steady voice in my life. Someone who ministers to me without even trying. ^1 Someone whose presence reminds me that God sends people exactly when we need them.

He thinks he was just sharing his story that day. He doesn't realize he was saving my life.

Some rides end at the destination. But some rides… they stay with you.

CHAPTER THIRTEEN: THE LAST ONE STANDING

He approached the car like a man walking through a world that no longer made sense. His steps were slow, uneven — not from physical pain, but from the weight of memories pressing down on him. When he opened the door, he didn't simply enter. He collapsed into the seat, like grief had hollowed him out from the inside. "Evening," he whispered, voice thin. Whisky Blu nodded gently. "Evening, brother." The car pulled away from the curb, and silence settled in — not empty, but full. Full of something unspoken, something trembling, something waiting to be released. A few minutes passed before the man exhaled a long, broken breath. "I don't talk much," he said. "But tonight… I just needed to be around someone who's alive." Whisky didn't turn around. He didn't push. He just listened — the way he always does, with his whole spirit. The man swallowed hard. "I'm the last one left in my family." The words cracked open something in the air. "My mom… she passed first. Ovarian cancer." He paused, eyes filling. "She had a partial hysterectomy years before. Thought she was safe. Thought she beat it. But cancer doesn't care about what you've already survived." He wiped his face with the sleeve of his jacket. "She fought. God, she fought. But it still took her." He stared out the window, watching the night blur past. "Then my dad. Prostate cancer. He ignored the symptoms. Brushed them off. By the time he went to the doctor, it was everywhere. I watched him shrink into someone I barely recognized." His voice trembled. "And my brother… my oldest brother… kidney cancer. He was the strong one. The protector. The one who always told me everything would be alright." He shook his head slowly. "It took him fast. Too fast." Silence filled the car again — but this time it wasn't heavy. It was holy. "I used to have a whole family," he whispered. "A whole world. Now it's just me. No parents. No siblings. No one who remembers the same stories. No one who calls just to say, 'You good?'" Whisky's voice was soft, steady. "That's a lot for one heart to carry." The man nodded, tears falling freely. "I don't feel like I'm carrying it. I feel like it's carrying me. Dragging me. Some days I feel like I'm disappearing. Like I'm a ghost in my own life." Whisky let the words settle before speaking. "You're not disappearing. You're surviving. And surviving that much loss… that's strength most people will never understand." The man let out a shaky laugh — the kind that comes from a place deeper than humor. "You know what hurts the most?" he said. "I don't have anyone left who knows me from the beginning. No one who remembers my childhood. No one who knows what my laugh used to sound like before all this." Whisky nodded slowly. "Sometimes God sends new witnesses into our lives. People who show up out of nowhere but see us clearer than the ones who knew us forever." The man looked up, eyes meeting Whisky's in the mirror — searching, hoping, doubting. "You think God still sees me?" he whispered. Whisky didn't hesitate. "Brother… if God didn't see you, you wouldn't be in this car right now." The man blinked, stunned by the certainty in Whisky's voice. Whisky continued, his tone shifting — deeper, anchored, almost pastoral. "You ever notice how grief makes everything quiet? Not because God left… but because He's sitting closer. Sometimes the silence is Him holding you so tight you can't hear anything else." The man's lips trembled. "I haven't felt God in a long time." Whisky shook his head gently. "You felt Him tonight. You just didn't recognize Him." The man frowned. "When?" Whisky's voice softened to a whisper. "When you said you needed to be around someone who's alive. That wasn't loneliness talking. That was your spirit reaching for light." The man covered his face with both hands and sobbed — not the polite kind, not the controlled kind, but the kind that breaks something open so healing can finally enter. Whisky kept driving, letting the tears fall, letting the moment breathe. After a while, the man spoke again, voice raw. "I didn't think I'd make it through today." Whisky felt the weight of that confession. Not dramatic. Not exaggerated. Just truth. "You made it," Whisky said. "And you're not as alone as you think. God didn't leave you. He led you here." The man nodded slowly, tears still streaming. "Thank you," he whispered. "For letting me be human. For letting me be seen. For reminding me I'm still here." When they reached his destination, he didn't get out right away. He sat there, breathing, grounding himself, letting the moment settle into his bones. Finally, he stepped out of the car and stood under the streetlight — a man with no family left, but somehow not alone. Still standing. Still breathing. Still held. Whisky watched him walk away, knowing this ride didn't erase the grief. But it gave him something he hadn't had in a long time: A spiritual touch. A reminder of presence. A moment where God whispered through a stranger, "I still see you." Another real moment. Another real ride. Another reminder that even the last one standing is never truly alone.

CHAPTER FOURTEEN: THE PREACHER WHO KEPT HIS SONG

The request came in on a Sunday afternoon — the kind of day when church bells ring across the city and people spill out of sanctuaries dressed in their best.

Whisky Blu pulled up to a quiet street where an old brick church stood at the corner, its stained-glass windows glowing in the sun.

But the man waiting on the curb wasn't coming from service.

He stood there with a small suitcase, a Bible tucked under his arm, and a voice that carried both strength and sorrow.

He opened the door and slid into the back seat.

"You Whisky?" he asked.

"Yes sir," Whisky replied. "Where we headed?"

The man hesitated.

"Somewhere with peace.

Anywhere that ain't here."

Whisky nodded and pulled away from the curb.

A few minutes into the ride, the man spoke — voice warm, melodic, the kind of voice that sounded like it had preached to thousands.

"I used to pastor that church," he said quietly.

"Twenty-three years.

Baptized babies.

Buried elders.

Sang every Sunday until the walls shook."

Whisky glanced at him in the mirror.

"What happened?"

The man swallowed hard.

"They found out I've been with women and umm… men. I'm pansexual."

Silence filled the car — not heavy, but respectful.

He continued.

"I didn't cheat.

Didn't lie.

Didn't hurt nobody.

I just told the truth about who I am.

And suddenly… the man who prayed for them, sang for them, stood with them…

became the man they feared."

Whisky nodded slowly.

"That kind of loss hits deep."

The man's eyes glistened.

"They said I couldn't lead no more.

Said I was an abomination.

Said God couldn't use me."

He let out a breath that trembled at the edges.

"But they forgot something," he said, voice growing steadier.

"They didn't call me.

God did."

Whisky felt that.

The man continued.

"I may have lost the building…

 but I didn't lose my voice.

 Didn't lose my calling.

Didn't lose my anointing.

 Didn't lose my song."

He looked out the window, watching the city roll by.

"You know what hurts the most?" he said softly.

 "I loved them.

 Still do.

 But I finally realized…

 I can't shrink myself to fit inside someone else's fear."

Whisky nodded.

 "That's truth right there."

As they approached a quiet park, the man leaned forward.

"Can you stop here?

 I like to sit by the water.

 Helps me remember that God's bigger than any church door that closes."

Whisky pulled in gently.

Before he stepped out, the man paused.

"Thank you," he said.

"For not looking at me like I'm broken.

For seeing the preacher… not the problem."

Whisky met his eyes in the mirror.

"You're not a problem.

You're a man who told the truth.

And sometimes… truth costs.

But it also frees."

The man smiled — a real smile, full of quiet strength.

He stepped out, Bible in hand, voice humming a soft hymn as he walked toward the water.

Whisky watched him go, knowing this ride wasn't about leaving a church.

It was about stepping into authenticity.

Some rides carry people away from rejection.

Others carry them toward the life they were always meant to live.

CHAPTER FIFTEEN: THE RIDER BEHIND THE MASK

Some rides begin like any other. But every now and then, a ride starts that you don't realize is about to change your life — or follow you into the next chapter of it.

It was late when he stepped into my car, carrying two versions of himself: the public persona the world adored, and the private man who was quietly falling apart.

He exhaled deeply. "Man… I'm tired."

"Long night?" I asked.

He shook his head. "Long life."

He wasn't performing. He wasn't posing. He wasn't the man the world thought he was.

He was just… human.

As we talked, he opened up about the pressure of living a double life, the fear of being seen, the exhaustion of pretending. And then he said something that hit deeper than he knew.

"You know… men like me always end up talking to men like you. I don't know why. It's like we're drawn to you. Like you see something in us we're scared to see, in ourselves."

I didn't respond right away. Because I knew exactly what he meant.

It wasn't the first time a man living behind a mask had opened up to me. It wasn't the first time someone who looked confident on the outside was unraveling on the inside. And it wasn't the first time a man felt safe enough to reveal the parts of himself he hid from the world.

When we reached his stop, he hesitated before getting out.

"You ever work out?" he asked suddenly.

I laughed. "Not like I should."

He smirked. "I can help with that. I train people on the side. Real training. Not the stuff people think I do."

I raised an eyebrow. "You're offering to train me?"

He nodded. "Yeah. Something tells me you need someone in your corner. And I… I think I need someone in mine."

I didn't know then how serious he was. I didn't know that the next time I saw him, he'd be standing in front of me in a fitted athletic shirt that showed the kind of physique people pay to look at — broad shoulders, defined chest, arms carved from discipline and survival, not vanity.

I didn't know that he'd push me, challenge me, and speak life into me in ways he didn't even realize.

I didn't know that training sessions would turn into conversations, conversations into trust, trust into a bond neither of us expected.

And I definitely didn't know that one day, during a late-night session when the gym was empty, and the air felt charged with something neither of us had language for, he would look at me with a seriousness I'd never seen in him before and say:

"There's something I need to tell you… but I don't know how."

I didn't ask. I didn't push. I just waited.

He took a breath, stepped closer — close enough that I could feel the heat of his body, close enough that the air between us felt different — and then he said:

"Not here. Not tonight. But soon."

He walked away before I could respond.

And that was the moment I realized:

This story wasn't finished. Not even close.

Some rides end when the door closes. Some friendships settle into place. But some connections… they pull you forward into something deeper, something unspoken, something waiting.

CHAPTER SIXTEEN: THE MILLIONAIRE WHO SAW THE VISION

Some rides feel ordinary until the moment they don't. Some passengers step into your car and step right back out. But every now and then, someone enters your life through the backseat and leaves a mark that shifts your entire future.

This was that ride.

I pulled up to a quiet, upscale neighborhood — the kind where the houses sit behind manicured hedges, and silence feels expensive. I was still renting a vehicle for $433 a week, grinding every day, rebuilding my life from homelessness with nothing but determination and a vision.

A vision for the BLU Family. A vision for The House of BLU. A vision for people who had fallen on hard times and needed a place to rise again.

When the passenger stepped into the car, he looked like any other businessman — tailored suit, calm presence, eyes that studied everything without revealing anything.

"Good afternoon," he said, settling into the backseat.

"Afternoon," I replied.

We drove in silence for a moment before he spoke again.

"You're Whisky Blu, correct?"

I glanced at him through the mirror. "That's me."

He nodded slowly, like he'd been waiting to confirm it.

"I've heard about you."

I raised an eyebrow. "From who?"

He smiled — a small, knowing smile. "People talk. Especially when someone is doing something that matters." I didn't respond. He continued.

"I heard you're rebuilding your life from the ground up. That you were homeless not long ago. That you're renting a car every week just to keep working."

I swallowed. "Something like that."

"And I heard," he added, "that you're trying to buy a home. Not for yourself — but to start something called the BLU Family. A place for people who've fallen on hard times. A place where they can rebuild with dignity."

I felt my chest tighten. Not from fear — from being seen.

"Who told you all that?" I asked.

He leaned forward slightly.

"Whisky… when someone carries a vision as big as yours, the universe makes sure the right people hear about it."

didn't know what to say.

He continued, voice calm but intentional.

"You're not just driving to survive. You're driving to build something. Something that will outlive you. Something that will change lives."

We rode in silence for a moment before he spoke again.

"Tell me about The House of BLU."

I hesitated, then opened up — not with a pitch, but with truth.

"It's a place for people who've fallen on hard times," I said. "A place where they can live, rebuild, find community, find purpose. A place where dignity is restored."

He nodded slowly.

"And the fleet?" he asked.

"I want to buy vehicles," I said. "Not for me — but for others. So they can work. So they can rebuild their lives. So they don't have to rent like I did."

He sat back, studying me.

"You're thinking bigger than most people who have ten times your resources."

I shrugged. "Some visions don't wait for money."

He smiled again — this time with something like respect.

When we reached his destination, he didn't get out right away. Instead, he reached into his briefcase and pulled out a sealed envelope.

"This is for you," he said. "Open it after I leave."

"What is it?" I asked.

"Seed," he said simply. "For the vision."

He stepped out, closed the door gently, and walked away.

I opened the envelope.

Inside was a letter — handwritten — and a certified document.

An endowment. A real one. Large enough to:

- purchase multiple vehicles

- start a fleet

- stop renting

- hire and empower others

- give people jobs, dignity, and stability

- and begin laying the foundation for The House of BLU

My hands shook as I read the letter:

"Whisky, Purpose recognizes purpose. Build the BLU Family. Build The House of BLU. And when the doors open... I'll return."

I sat in that car and cried — not from sadness, but from recognition. From the realization that God had sent provision through a stranger who wasn't a stranger at all.

He was part of the story. Part of the movement. Part of the foundation.

That endowment didn't just change my life. It changed the lives of the people who would one day drive those vehicles. People rebuilding their dignity. People finding stability. People rediscovering their worth.

It changed the lives of the people who would one day walk through the doors of The House of BLU.

Some rides end at the drop-off. Some rides become memories.

But some rides... they become miracles.

This was one of them.

CHAPTER SEVENTEEN: THE GCAP REVELATION

People see the BLU Movement now — the vision, the purpose, the fleet, the community, the hope — and they think it started with success.

It didn't.

It started in a small room at GCAP — **Greater Community AIDS Project** — a transitional house for people living with HIV.

GCAP was supposed to be a stepping stone. A temporary place to stabilize. A two-year limit. A communal living environment where everyone was trying to rebuild.

And I was one of them.

I was living there when I started renting a vehicle for $433 a week just so I could drive rideshare.

People thought I was crazy. But I wasn't trying to get rich. I was trying to get free.

I was trying to pull myself up by my bootstraps — even when the boots were worn out, even when the straps were thin, even when the world said it wasn't possible.

And every day I drove, I met people who reminded me why I couldn't give up.

The wheelchair rider who spoke life into me. The man behind the mask who found safety in my presence. The millionaire who saw my purpose before I had the resources to fulfill it. The broken, the healing, the searching, the rising.

Every ride was a sermon. Every passenger was a mirror. Every mile was a step toward something I didn't yet have language for.

But GCAP… GCAP was the soil where the seed was planted.

Not because it was perfect. Not because it had all the answers. But because it showed me the gap.

GCAP offered temporary shelter — but not long-term stability.

It offered community — but not permanence.

It offered support — but not a future.

And none of that was because the board didn't care. They cared deeply. They meant well.

But they lacked something essential:

Lived experience.

Except me.

I was the only board member who had lived the life the residents were living. I knew what it felt like to lose everything. I knew what it felt like to rebuild from nothing. I knew what it felt like to be grateful for a bed while still knowing you had nowhere to go when your two years were up.

And that's when the vision hit me:

"If GCAP can help people survive… then The House of BLU will help people LIVE."

Not just people living with HIV. Not just people in transitional housing. Not just people who fit a category.

But anyone who had fallen on hard times. Anyone who had lost family. Anyone who had been pushed aside, forgotten, or left to figure it out alone.

A home that didn't expire. A community that didn't rotate people out. A family that didn't end after two years.

A place where people could become the best version of themselves.

That night, sitting in my room at GCAP, I realized:

GCAP wasn't the destination. It was the birthplace.

The birthplace of the BLU Family. The birthplace of The House of BLU. The birthplace of a movement bigger than me.

And the rides you've read about in this book — the miracles, the persons, the moments, the millionaire — they weren't random.

They were confirmation.

They were alignment. They were divine timing. They were the universe saying:

"You're ready. Now build it."

And that's exactly what I did.

CHAPTER EIGHTEEN (FINALE): THE RIDE THAT CAUGHT ME BY SURPRISE

The request came in close to midnight — the kind of hour when the world feels thinner, when truth sits closer to the surface.

Whisky Blu pulled up to a dimly lit street where the streetlights flickered like they were nervous.

A young man stepped out of the shadows.

Not walking.

Not rushing.

Just… existing.

Like someone who'd been holding his breath for years.

He opened the door and slid into the back seat without a word.

"You Whisky?" he asked quietly.

"Yes sir," Whisky replied. "Where we headed?"

The man hesitated — eyes darting to the rearview mirror, then to the window, then back to his hands.

"I don't know," he whispered.

"I just… I need to get away."

Whisky nodded.

"Alright. We'll drive."

They pulled off, the city falling away behind them.

Minutes passed in silence — the kind of silence that isn't empty, but full of something unspoken.

Finally, the man exhaled.

"My family thinks I'm dead," he said.

Whisky's hands tightened on the wheel — not from fear, but from instinct.

The man continued.

"I left home five years ago.

No goodbye.

No explanation.

Just… disappeared."

Whisky didn't interrupt.

"I wasn't running from them," the man said.

"I was running from what happened.

From what I saw.

From what I survived."

His voice trembled — not weak, but haunted.

"I've been living under a different name.

Different city.

Different life.

But tonight… something happened.

Something that reminded me of everything I tried to bury."

Whisky kept driving — slow, steady, present.

The man leaned forward, voice barely above a whisper.

"I think someone found me."

The air in the car shifted — thickened — like the moment before a storm breaks.

"I don't know who to trust," he said.

 "I don't know where to go.

 But when I saw your name pop up on the app… something told me to get in."

Whisky met his eyes in the mirror.

"You're safe in this car," he said.

 "We'll figure it out."

The man swallowed hard.

"You don't understand," he whispered.

 "If they found me…

 they'll come."

Whisky didn't flinch.

"Then we keep moving."

The man stared at him — searching, measuring, hoping.

"You believe me?" he asked.

Whisky nodded.

"I've carried enough stories in this seat to know when someone's telling the truth."

The man exhaled — a breath that sounded like release and fear tangled together.

"Then take me somewhere they'll never think to look."

Whisky turned the wheel — not toward the highway, not toward the city, but toward the unknown.

The night swallowed them whole.

And somewhere in the darkness, a new story began.

A story too big for one book.

Too deep for one volume.

Too dangerous to end here ….

CLOSING REFLECTIONS

When I first sat behind the wheel, I didn't know the road would become my teacher. I didn't know strangers would become mirrors. I didn't know the quiet hum of the engine would become a soundtrack to stories that would reshape me in ways I'm still discovering.

Long before these rides, I stood behind a pulpit at Oasis of Love Ministries — a pastor on the cutting edge, creating a space for the ostracized, the marginalized, the rejected, the distressed, and the misunderstood. I didn't know then that life would require me to walk through the very valleys I once guided others through. I didn't know that the calling to help the homeless would one day become my own lived reality. I didn't know that becoming HIV-positive and losing everything would be the soil where a new purpose would take root.

But the road has a way of bringing you full circle.

Every ride in this book — every whispered confession, every moment of courage, every tear, every laugh — reminded me of something simple and sacred:

People are carrying more than we can see. And sometimes, all they need is a safe place to set it down for a moment.

These stories are not just about the passengers who stepped into my car. They're about all of us — the parts we hide, the truths we carry, the battles we fight in silence, and the hope we cling to even when life feels heavy.

If there's one thing I've learned from the road, it's this:

Healing doesn't always happen in hospitals or churches or therapy rooms. Sometimes it happens in motion — in the space between where we've been and where we're going.

Volume I is a collection of those moments. Moments that held me.

Moments that taught me. Moments that reminded me that humanity is still alive, still tender, still worth believing in.

But the journey isn't over.

There are stories I haven't told yet — stories too deep, too raw, too unfinished to fit inside these pages. Stories still unfolding in the rearview mirror of my life. Stories that will demand more honesty, more courage, and more truth than I've ever shared before.

Volume II is waiting. And when the time comes, it will not whisper. It will speak loudly. Boldly. Unapologetically.

Until then, thank you for riding with me. Thank you for listening. Thank you for seeing the people behind the stories — and the man behind the wheel.

The road continues. And so do we.

TEASER FOR VOLUME II

Stories From The Rideshare Driver's Seat – Volume II

The Road Gets Darker. The Truth Gets Deeper. The Stories Get Realer.

Every story in Volume I brought you closer to the heart of the road — the quiet confessions, the whispered truths, the moments that changed people in the span of a ride.

But some stories don't end when the car stops. Some stories follow you home. Some stories wait in the shadows. Some stories refuse to stay buried.

Whisky Blu knows this better than most.

Long before he became a rideshare driver, he stood behind a pulpit at Oasis of Love Ministries — a pastor ahead of his time, creating a sanctuary for the ostracized, the marginalized, the rejected, the distressed, and the misunderstood. He didn't know then that the very people he fought to protect would one day mirror his own journey. He dreamed of helping the homeless… only to become homeless himself. He preached healing… only to face his own diagnosis of HIV. He built a refuge for the broken… only to discover that he, too, would need refuge.

What felt like loss was preparation. What felt like a collapse was foundation. What felt like the end was only the beginning.

And now, the road is calling him deeper.

The young man from the midnight ride — the one whose family believed he was dead — didn't disappear after that night. His story didn't close with the door of the car. It opened something bigger. Something darker. Something that pulled Whisky Blu into a world he never expected to enter.

Volume II picks up where the night left off — with unanswered questions, hidden dangers, and a truth that refuses to stay quiet.

In the next volume, you'll encounter:

- stories that test the limits of compassion
- riders running from more than heartbreak
- secrets that carry real consequences
- moments where safety, faith, and instinct collide
- and a mystery that stretches far beyond a single ride

The road ahead is not gentle. It is not predictable. It is not safe.

But it is necessary.

Because some stories demand to be told. Some lives depend on being heard. And some journeys don't just change the passengers — they change the driver.

Volume II is coming. And when it arrives... you'll understand why the last ride of Volume I was only the beginning.

ABOUT THE AUTHOR

Whisky Blu is a storyteller, a minister, an advocate, and a witness to the quiet truths people carry.

For more than forty years, he has served communities through ministry, mentorship, and compassionate leadership — always centering dignity, humanity, and the belief that every person's story deserves to be heard.

His journey has taken him through seasons of caregiving, loss, reinvention, homelessness, and healing.

Those experiences didn't break him — they sharpened his vision, deepened his empathy, and shaped the voice that now guides his work.

As a rideshare driver, Whisky discovered something unexpected:

the back seat of a car can become a sanctuary.

A place where strangers speak their truth.

A place where stories unfold without judgment.

A place where healing begins in the space between two people who may never meet again.

Stories From The Rideshare Driver's Seat is born from those moments — fictionalized to protect privacy, but rooted in the real humanity he encounters every day.

Whisky writes with the heart of a minister, the honesty of a survivor, and the soul of someone who has lived enough life to know that everyone carries something unseen.

Beyond storytelling, Whisky Blu is the co-host and co-creator of CONVERSATIONS w/ Whisky Blu & Eric Too, a YouTube series dedicated to unity, healing, and real dialogue.

He also operates a private driver service built on care, professionalism, and the belief that every ride is an opportunity to make someone's day lighter.

Whisky's mission is simple:

to build community through truth, compassion, and the power of shared experience.

Volume I is just the beginning.

The road ahead — and the stories waiting to be told — promise even more depth, intensity, and humanity in the volumes to come.

BACK-OF-BOOK SUMMARY

Step into the passenger seat of a rideshare car where every mile carries a story, and every stranger holds a truth waiting to be heard.

In Stories From The Rideshare Driver's Seat – Volume I, Whisky Blu opens the door to a world where his vehicle becomes a sanctuary on wheels, and the back seat becomes a confessional. Through eighteen powerful, fictionalized stories inspired by real encounters, this book explores the raw, unfiltered humanity of people navigating illness, identity, grief, survival, reinvention, and hope.

But this book is more than the stories of others — It is the story of a man who has come full circle.

Long before he became a rideshare driver, Whisky Blu served as the pastor of Oasis of Love Ministries — a visionary leader ahead of his time, creating a spiritual home for the ostracized, the marginalized, the rejected, the distressed, and the misunderstood. He didn't know then that the very people he fought for would one day mirror his own journey. He dreamed of helping the homeless… only to become homeless himself. He preached healing… only to face his own diagnosis of HIV. He built a refuge for the broken… only to discover that he, too, would need refuge.

What felt like loss was preparation. What felt like a collapse was foundation. What felt like the end was the beginning of something greater.

Now, behind the wheel, Whisky Blu encounters riders whose stories echo the very struggles he survived. Meet the woman fighting breast cancer with quiet courage. The preacher who lost his congregation but not his calling. The man behind the mask who reveals more than he intends. The millionaire who sees a vision worth funding. The client of GCAP's Transitional house who becomes a board member and alumni who discovers his purpose. And the rider whose family believed he was dead — a moment that changes everything.

These are not just rides. They are moments of truth — intimate, emotional, and unforgettable.

Whisky Blu writes with the heart of a minister, the honesty of a survivor, and the soul of someone who has lived enough life to understand that everyone carries something unseen. His stories remind us that healing can happen anywhere... even in the back seat of a car.

Volume I is only the beginning. The final chapter opens a door into a deeper, more gripping journey — one that will leave readers breathless and longing for Volume II.

Real people. Real moments. Real stories. And the road ahead is just getting started.